Ian Takes Flight

Written and Illustrated by Richard Nattoo
Edited by Olivia Wilmot

SAPLING BOOKS

Cover design by Richard Nattoo.
Interior illustrations by Richard Nattoo.

ISBN: 9780985375546
Library of Congress Control Number: 2020947053

Published by Sapling Books, an imprint of Bookman Express, LLC.
For publishing inquiries, email works@bookmanexpress.pub.
For general inquiries, email info@bookmanexpress.pub.
www.bookmanexpress.pub

**BOOKMAN
EXPRESS**

| BEX0006 |

To my Mother, Miss Frennie and Marlon.

It was the summer and Ian was spending time with his godmother.

He always liked coming to visit. He could spend time with the trees. He could make his small gardens in the bushes. The plants were his friends.

Every morning, after breakfast, he would do his chores and head out to his garden under the big apple tree in the bushes. "Hey! The corn is growing!" Ian chuckled. He could only see soil at that spot yesterday.

"Ian! Come and bathe and eat your dinner!" his godmother called out. A full day had passed by. Approaching the house, Ian could see the beautiful sunset. He felt warm.

"See you tomorrow, Sun," he said. The sun was his friend, too.

Ian took one last look at the changing colours in the sky and ran inside. What magic would tomorrow bring?

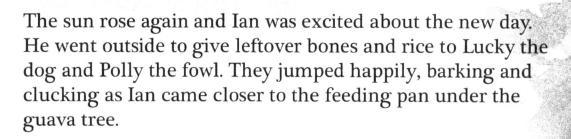

The sun rose again and Ian was excited about the new day. He went outside to give leftover bones and rice to Lucky the dog and Polly the fowl. They jumped happily, barking and clucking as Ian came closer to the feeding pan under the guava tree.

"I'm happy to see you too," said Ian. He couldn't wait to go check on his corn though. "Maybe I'll bring Polly and Lucky along with me today," he mused.

Ian, Lucky and Polly arrived at the apple tree to check up on the corn but, instead, they got a surprise. Mother Nature had left them a bright, pink carpet! It was apple season and the tree was in full bloom, dropping magical blossoms everywhere. All three stared in amazement.

"Wow..." said Ian.

All of a sudden, the trio heard a rustling in the bushes.
What could it be? They looked closely at the spot where
the sound came from.

Ian squinted his eyes...

...he leaned forward...

...and *zip!* The chase was on!

The critter took off at light speed and the troop ran as fast as they could to catch it. What was it? It seemed to be playing! Lucky, Polly and Ian ran and ran and ran until they were right back where they started, at the foot of the apple tree.

Ian saw the leaves shake. "It must be up there!"

So, up the apple tree Ian went. He wasn't giving up. Polly and Lucky sat at the roots and watched Ian clamber up the branches.

"You think you're fast? Just watch," Ian thought as he climbed.

Ian continued way up in the thick of the tree until it was pitch black. He didn't know what to do. Then something magical happened.

"Ian," a voice called out.

"Hello?" Ian replied.

A bright light appeared along with something else that spoke to Ian – a mongoose.

"My name is Eli, the High-goose of *The Place Beyond the Sky*. You have a good heart, Ian, and that means you can enter. Take this star and keep climbing until you see the light."

"See you on the other side," said Eli as he scurried away and disappeared into the darkness.

Ian sat still for a moment, then decided to make his way onward. Carefully, he climbed.

Ian went up the apple tree until his head popped out of a hole in the ground. How was this even possible? He was just in a tree! He saw Lucky, Polly and Eli but they were different somehow. And they were arguing about something.

Wait. Were they all talking? Ian stayed put and listened. He heard Lucky ask, "Are you sure this is a good idea, Eli? To bring him here?"

"He has the heart for this place," Eli replied. "He should see it."

The three caught sight of the boy and called him closer, so Ian went. He had so many questions but Eli spoke first.

"This is *The Place Beyond the Sky*," he announced.

"This world is magic," Lucky declared. "And limitless."

"That star is your key," Polly told him. "Keep it close!"

"We're here to guide you, Ian," Lucky said. "We'll help to make sure you always get back, okay? Plus, adventures are more fun with friends!"

"Just remember," warned Eli. "Don't come here alone."

Lucky, Polly and Eli stared at Ian, waiting for him to speak. Ian blinked. He could barely whisper, "I… I can't believe this."

"Well then," Eli drew closer. "Let's explore!"

They took flight!

Ian was stunned. He held on tighter to Eli as they all soared higher and higher into the majestic atmosphere.

"Wow!" Ian yelled with excitement. "This is like the kite festival Mummy took me to!"

"These are kite-rays," Eli told him. The kite-rays waved at the four visitors. Amazing!

Ian caught wondrous glimpses of magic as they flew.

"Was that a whale?" He almost couldn't believe it.

"Entire worlds meet in *The Place Beyond the Sky*, Ian," said Eli.

This was like a dream.

Astounding creatures met them along the way, each one like a world on its own. Ian saw colours shimmer all along the tail of a cloud-fish as lights glowed deep in its body. It looked like a whole new sky was in there.

"Watch out, Eli!" cried Ian. "Mind we go too far!"

"Steady yourself, Ian," Polly said. "We'll go as far as your heart will take us!"

Ian took deep breaths. He could feel his heart pounding steadily like a drum. He started to feel brave. "Go higher, Eli!"

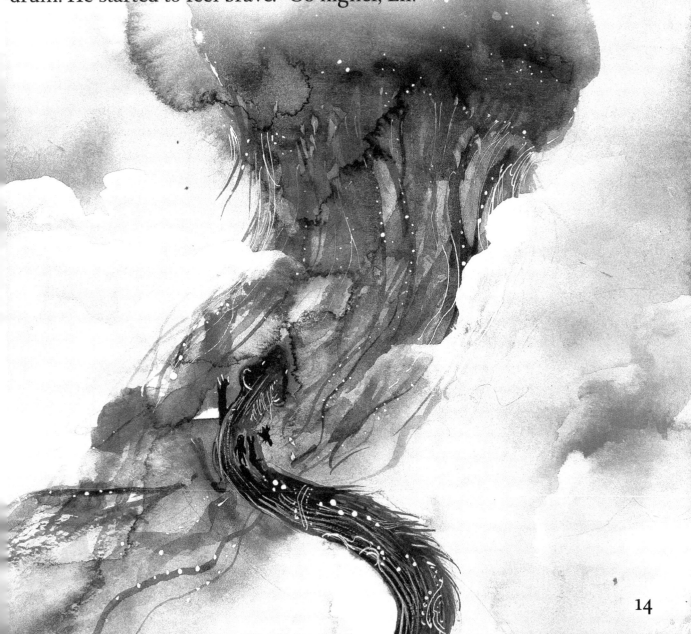

Ian saw the large, mysterious being he glimpsed earlier. It really was a whale – an extraordinary one! Ian opened his eyes wide.

"A flying forest! Can we go there?" The great whale floated in the air, waiting for them to land on its back.

"Together, we can!" said Lucky.

"To the magic!" Eli laughed.

They raced in the cool mist of the flying forest. The trees seemed to sing! Peppermint breeze wrapped around Ian and gave him a hug. The four of them spent the whole day there.

"Let's race again!" Ian called.

But the sun was setting. Eli smiled. "We have to leave now, Ian."

Ian smiled, too. "Okay."

Ian told his friends goodbye and took the star from his pocket to return it to Eli.

"Keep it, my friend," said Eli. "Remember, you will need it to get down the apple tree and to visit again."

"I can't wait!" Ian exclaimed. He put the star back in his pocket, entered the hole and climbed all the way down until he got to his garden.

Everything looked normal again as far as Ian could tell. Lucky and Polly greeted him while Eli scampered off. He gave Polly and Lucky a cuddle. "Thanks for being my friends."

Ian happily went back to his godmother in time for dinner. What a day!

Later, as Ian drifted off to sleep, he could feel his body rock and sway.

Each new day was so exciting! Every morning after breakfast and chores, Ian, Lucky and Polly would meet Eli under the apple tree. Then their adventures would begin!

They flew to far away places, spending hours playing in the new worlds they discovered. Nothing seemed impossible in *The Place Beyond the Sky*. The creatures were magnificent and their kindness made them more beautiful.

Some days were slow and sweet, reminding Ian of things like:
   his granny's sweet potato pudding;
     his godmother's chocolate tea;
       or finally getting to open a present.

Some days were as swift as the wind! Sports day races could never compare to this. Together, they charged ahead with the sky-horses, even faster than Usain Bolt!

Ian was so happy. He felt free!

The Place Beyond the Sky was starting to feel like home to Ian.

"A manatee!" he exclaimed.

"You mean mamatee," noted Polly.

He had seen pictures of these gentle giants on posters at school. He would always look out for them when his father took him fishing.

Ian loved every moment here.

But the end of summer came. It was the last day of Ian's stay at his godmother's house. He started the morning as usual but, after feeding Lucky and Polly, he had to go inside to pack. Ian's mother and father were coming to pick him up later.

Eli waited at the apple tree for Ian.

Ian didn't come.

24

It was evening by the time Ian finished packing. His parents hadn't arrived yet, so he rushed out to the yard to find his friends. Ian couldn't bear the idea of leaving them without saying goodbye but Polly was asleep and he couldn't find Lucky anywhere. So, he went to the apple tree by himself to look for Eli.

Eli wasn't there.

Ian just had to say goodbye. Maybe he could find his friends in *The Place Beyond the Sky*? What else could he do?

Ian began climbing the tree.

When Ian arrived at *The Place Beyond the Sky*, it felt strange. It was too quiet without his friends' company. Where were they? "I better find them fast," Ian thought.

Without Eli to fly with, Ian wasn't sure which way to go. He walked through a curious forest, amazed by the rainbow fireflies that lit the way for him. Maybe this wasn't so bad after all.

Soon, Ian reached a big field. On the other side stood a lone tree. He almost felt like it was pulling him.

"To the tree!" Ian declared.

Ian ran all the way across the field to the tree. He was sure his friends were over there.

When Ian got there, he wasn't alone. There was an extraordinary bird at the top of this tall, towering tree. He could feel the powerful gaze of the bird. Ian swallowed.

"Were *you* calling me?" He didn't dare to ask out loud.

Looking closer at the tree, he saw that it had a cave underneath it. Were his friends inside?

Ian looked up at the bird again. It spread its wings as if to say, "You may enter."

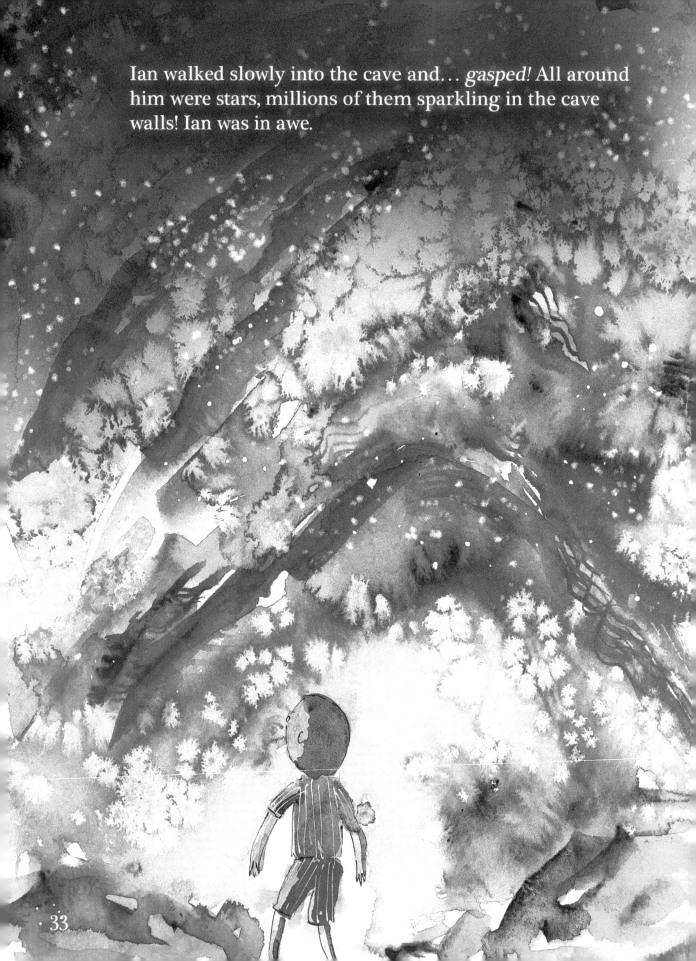

Ian walked slowly into the cave and… *gasped!* All around him were stars, millions of them sparkling in the cave walls! Ian was in awe.

All the stars began to glow brighter. One by one, the stars broke free from the cave walls, swirling together in a beautiful mist. Ian felt his pocket getting hot and realized that his star was shining brighter too. The star lifted out of Ian's pocket and spiralled with the others. It was mesmerizing.

After some time, the stars began to flicker and dim. Then they all started drifting back to the cave walls - and Ian's star was drifting away with them!

"Uh oh!" Ian was alarmed. He tried to catch it but he couldn't. Like a butterfly, the star would escape just before Ian could get it. "Oh no!" Ian cried, "Help!"

That's when he remembered what Eli said: *don't come here alone.* No one was coming to help. No one knew where he was. "I should have never come here by myself," Ian thought. "What if I can't get my star back? I want to go home!"

Right away, Ian took off his shirt and used it as a net to catch his star. He got it! Ian bundled the prize close to his chest and ran out of the cave as fast as he could. When he got outside, it was almost entirely dark except for his star glowing inside his shirt.

As Ian looked up to see if the bird was still there, it flew away.

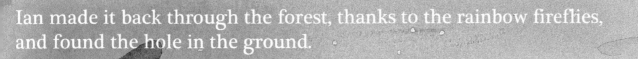

Ian made it back through the forest, thanks to the rainbow fireflies, and found the hole in the ground.

Soon, he was safely at his godmother's house again.
Ian's father embraced him as soon as he saw him.
His godmother was busy gifting bananas, yam, mangos and other treasures to his mother as they talked joyfully about the days past and the days ahead.

Ian felt comforted seeing family again and he was very thankful to be on his way home.

A year passed since all the great adventures. The holidays came and it was time for Ian to stay at his godmother's house again. He still had his star and he was so excited! Ian really wanted to go back to *The Place Beyond the Sky*. He wanted to play with Eli, Lucky and Polly. He would tell them how sorry he was that he didn't say goodbye. He really wanted to tell Eli about what happened in the cave.

As soon as Ian got to his godmother's house, he set off for the apple tree.

The tree wasn't there.

Ian was confused. His stomach hurt. Had it been cut down? Where were the roots?

He needed answers.

Ian ran to his godmother and asked her about the tree.

"What apple tree?" she replied. "The only apple tree in this yard is from when I was a little girl. It got struck by lightning a long time ago, Ian. You must mean the mango tree further down."

Ian felt cold. He was speechless...

...and very sad.

"Ian," his godmother held him tight. "Guess what? I took care of your corn while you were gone. I even planted back some. Go and look at them, and take the dog and that fowl with you. They must miss you."

Ian felt a little better when he saw Lucky and Polly. When he saw that Lucky had a puppy and Polly had a brood of chicks, Ian couldn't help but laugh and hug them.

"Come, Lucky. Come, Polly," said Ian. "Let's go look for the apple tree."

As they came to the place where the apple tree used to be, Ian saw how strong and mighty his corn now was. The stalks were huge! He searched through the corn patch for any sign of the apple tree.

Only corn.

Ian took an ear of corn and stripped it to feed Polly's chicks. Would he ever see Eli again?

Ian looked up at the friendly sky. Birds sailed through the air. A mango tree swayed in the distance. The sun shone brightly. Ian felt warm.

"Let's race!" he said to Lucky and Polly.
This was going to be a good holiday.

But wait.

What was that growing by the bushes?

Jamaican visual artist Richard Nattoo has loved art since he was very young, showing great interest in colour, texture, form and shape. He enjoys creating surreal, dreamlike images that explore different human emotions. His works have been displayed at various premier exhibitions at the National Gallery of Jamaica since 2012. *Ian Takes Flight* is Richard's first published book.

Olivia Wilmot has loved stories, music and nature since childhood when she could always be found writing, singing and exploring outdoors. Trained in education and social sciences, she loves engaging in projects that help keep the magic of childhood alive. She writes, creates music and teaches. Olivia enjoys spending time with her family and living in her island home, Jamaica.

Are you ready for more fun with Ian, Lucky and Polly? Ask a parent or responsible adult to help you scan this QR code for interactive activities, updates and more adventures with Ian.

You can also visit www.bookmanexpress.pub/iantakesflight

CPSIA information can be obtained
at www.ICGtesting.com
Printed in the USA
BVHW022257241120
593916BV00003BA/25